Lofty prisons big and tall,
Lofty Prisons short and small.
No money for prisons,
that's the rub; the hue stays on,
even when you scrub.
Gone are now the prison walls,
gone also are the rooms and halls.
Just a tree or shrub survives,
you work like hell to stay alive.

Blue Man

J.J. Smiley

Published by J.J. Smiley, 2022.

BLUE MAN

First edition. December 23, 2022.

Copyright © 2022 J.J. Smiley.

ISBN: 979-8215480304

Written by J.J. Smiley.

Table of Contents

To Judith my life companion and muse.

Chapter 1

Dennis had arranged to have the day off to take delivery of the antique car. The car itself was not that expensive. The certificates for ownership of a gasoline-powered auto plus the permits for purchase and use of the gasoline were twice the cost of the vehicle itself. Dennis recalled how much older men had reminisced about the feeling of power from the acceleration of a gas-powered vehicle, how it would push you back into the seat, how it would feel to accelerate from nothing to 60mph in just a few seconds. He couldn't wait to find the Federal Chemical Depot and use his permit to purchase the gasoline. It had taken most of the day to get through the purchasing paperwork, and if he were lucky, he would get some petroleum and be home by evening.

Gasoline wasn't the only juice flowing that evening as the car sped down the highway at well over a hundred miles per hour. The acceleration was everything he and his wife Dorothy had thought it would be, and the excitement brought on an erotic tingle in both of them.

The red antique, 2000 Jaguar convertible, flew into the corner of 'Dead Man's Curve,' a road that was barely acknowledged by a rusty sign along the edge of the pavement. The gasoline was expensive and hard to get, but the two people in the car were having the time of their life. Dennis had been driving and decided to see how the suspension of the old sports car would handle the tight arch in the road. The Jag's coil springs compressed, and the sway bar torqued as needed. The car drove perfectly. In the passenger seat, Dorothy was white-knuckled, hanging on for the ride.

A moving blur, a sickening thud, and the front window became a deranged spider's web. Dennis slammed on the brakes at the same instant Dorothy screamed. The wheels locked up and set the car sliding sideways on the asphalt. It began spinning but finally came to a halt just before hitting a small tree. The smell of burnt rubber filled the air; the car's engine had died.

Dennis and Dorothy got out and ran back to the spot where Dennis had hit the brakes. It was dark; there were no lampposts out on this deserted stretch of road. There was only the moon giving up its light grudgingly. They went back to the car. It wouldn't start, and Dorothy began calling the police on her cell phone.

"Do you think we should just call a tow truck instead?" Dennis said, looking somewhat scared.

"No, there might be an injured animal or something, besides we'll need a police report for the insurance," Dorothy replied.

"Don't worry, I'll tell them I was driving; all I had was a cola. But, of course, you always need to have your stinking Dewars!" She said sarcastically.

Remarkably, only ten minutes passed before the police showed up. Dennis and Dorothy, leaning on the Jag, explained the whole affair.

"I must have hit an animal. And the car won't run now, and we'll need a police report for the insurance." She told them.

The two police officers took their flashlights and began searching the area where the skid marks started. They found blood not far from where the brake marks first appeared on the highway. The blood trail led off the road and into the ditch. The ditch vegetation was crushed aside, and the trail of bent saw grass and reeds went up the other side of the ditch and into the woods.

The police, with Dennis and Dorothy trailing, entered the woods. The officers began fanning out to look for the animal. They would spend some time looking, but not too much.

One of the cops yelled, "Over here, it's a body... and it's dead".

Fear ran through the couple that only moments ago were thinking how great the night had started out. Dennis thought his bladder was going to release.

"No sweat, it's a Blue Man." The officer added.

Relief now readily replaced the fear in the young couple. Dennis' pants remained dry.

"It's bizarre. Blues don't ever come out this far. We're almost a half mile from the boundary road. The prisoners know, past that road, they can be shot by regular citizens, just for sport". The officer explained.

They all stared at the dark blue color of the man lying there. The blue was dark but contrasted in the moonlight with the bright red blood lying around him. They all wondered silently what crime this man might have committed to earn such a cruel fate.

"Well, there's nothing more to do here." The cop said, breaking the reverie. "It's almost ten o'clock; we need to get back." He said to his partner.

Once back on the road, the officer stopped Dorothy." It is obvious that you were going way too fast from the length of the skid marks." He said.

"I'll have to write you a ticket for that." Her jaw dropped in protest, but she held back any further response.

"We'll call in a tow truck for you." He finished. "Have a good night." The officer said, handing her the ticket with a big grin, and drove off.

Dorothy was pretty well seething by this point. However, she had given the police the story that she was the driver, so she got the ticket.

"There's no way I'm taking the blame for this." She told Dennis.

"Hey, it's only a minor infraction; what's the big deal?" He told her.

"Listen, I got caned once before, and it's no fun; even one swipe with the cane can buckle your knees. Of course, it depends on who's using the stick." She retorted in a seething huff.

"What the hell? I got the ticket. I'll get the cane, but you'll pay dearly for this, you nitwit." Dorothy told him.

The remnant smell of burnt rubber was nothing compared to the acrid smell of Dorothy's disgust permeating the night air.

Waiting for the tow truck, Dennis stared back at the woods.

"I'm just glad it was a Blue. If it hadn't been a criminal, We'd be up on charges of homicide. Maybe we'd wind up getting a Blue sentence ourselves." He said, half out loud.

"If homicide charges were the issue, this wouldn't be a WE situation, and you can bet on that," Dorothy openly commented.

The thought of his skin being genetically turned blue ran through his mind and made him sick to his stomach. He thought of being on the run for the rest of his life, being a legal target for anyone wanting to relieve their frustration. Severe beatings of Blues were more common than execution because most people couldn't find it in themselves to murder someone, even if they were blue. Nevertheless, to Dennis, a quick death seemed more humane. With no more prison buildings, what else could be done? How in the world did this ever come to be?

Chapter 2

Floyd thought about how much fun it was to work in a research lab. Never knowing what the next assignment would be. He had worked here since graduating as a chemist from a significant college. Most of all, the Human Relations department that hired him liked his highly motivated attitude. He was a team leader type, and his test scores showed a high degree of potential loyalty.

He had been working on a new food coloring that would enhance the color of a food and enhance the taste as well. Unfortunately, months had gone by with little forward movement on the project.

What was known so far was that the color change was permanent and not reversible. The only improvement was that the change took place at a molecular level and happened very fast but didn't change the taste at all. The last drawback was that the only color that could be attained was a darker shade of blue.

Floyd took his findings to the manager of the laboratory. He entered the manager's office and was greeted by Sean Mc Seamore. As Sean reached out to shake hands with Floyd, he was greeted by Floyd's completely blue hand. He quickly pulled his hand away, and Floyd, laughing, told him it was not contagious, and it absolutely won't rub off.

"I don't know what I 'm going to do. If it ends up covering my whole body, I'll look like an X-Men mutant."

"Jesus, Floyd, how long before you'll know?"

"A few more hours, I guess. It was taking about four hours for the monkeys to turn blue."

"Monkeys? Why were you testing monkeys? I thought this was for food enhancement."

"Correct, and who would be eating that genetically augmented food? People, right?"

"Yeah, your right. I don't know what I was thinking."

Floyd's face was darkening as they spoke, making Sean very nervous. They talked over the project details for more than an hour, and Floyd looked like a concord grape before it was over.

Everyone in the office could see that Floyd was blue as he returned to his lab. He didn't need a mirror. He could feel everyone's eyes on him as he passed. All he could see now was that *both* his hands were blue.

Sean knew that an agreement had been made between his company and the sister company Bloodwood but was unsure exactly how the arrangement would be finalized. What would food additives and a security company have in common anyway?

Chapter 3

The spin is in, thought Congressman Donald L. Doddson. Everything had gone according to plan. Doddson sat at his desk and poured himself a two-fingered glass of Old Grand-Dad Bourbon Whiskey, his favorite. Pleased with himself, he sipped from the glass as he sat looking out the window of his office. The bourbon had a slight tickling burn that he enjoyed as he swallowed. Through the office picture window, he could see the White House while sitting at his desk, and visions of grandeur of what the future might hold swirled in his head.

There was no reason to think he couldn't achieve a higher platform than his current congressional seat. He was from a state with no term limits and had held this position for many years. He was a persistent and persuasive personality and knew better than anyone the art of the deal.

There was a knock on the door; Doddson quickly finished his drink, stuck the glass and the bottle in the lower drawer, and calmly said, "Come in."

A young man appeared in the doorway. Chris Rogan was a congressional staff member and did extensive work exclusively for the congressman. He was clean-cut and well-dressed; Doddson often used him to aid in polishing off the hard sell deals. Chris knew the ins and outs of the Washington rat race and where and when to use the hard push and the easy payoff.

"Congressman," he said, "I've just gotten the news that your bill is going to the floor. I also have the final report on who will be voting with you to pass this bill. It should pass on tomorrow's vote and then be sent to the Senate floor. We also have all the assurances we need to pass the Senate. It's unlikely that the president would veto this bill in light of the current public opinion and rising crime rates."

"Thanks, Chris," the congressman said, "that'll be all for now."

Being dismissed, he excused himself and closed the door. He hated how the congressman would dismiss him so flagrantly rather than being kind enough to inquire about him or his family. He never felt appreciated, well paid, yes, but he never got that all-important pat on the back. Chris came from an average family. All his family members were moderately successful, both professionals and tradesmen. Chris had watched as the current administration had penalized success with overwhelming taxes and regulations. He was glad that he had decided years ago if you can't beat them, join them and, after college, went immediately into politics. He headed down the hallway, thinking that someday his time would come. Just be patient.

Doddson leaned back in the chair, pulled out his bottle and glass again, and continued with his self-indulgence. Couldn't be better, he thought; as soon as my bill passes, I'll start moving to bring in Bloodwood to begin drawing up security contracts to oversee the new system. He had met the head of Bloodwood at a fundraiser a few years back, and the CEO had planted the seed of this plan in his mind. He thought of the lucrative paybacks he would get from Bloodwood and Genetic Tech.

He first had to fight off Parks and Recreation as well as the Bureau of Land Management and Fish and Wildlife. They were not entirely hard battles to win because they all cost the taxpayers money and never paid for themselves; they were always asking for more budget. In addition, the large National Parks were entirely underutilized; only a small percentage of the population was ever in the parks, even though everyone paid for their upkeep.

Genetic Tech, of course, was the only company that would be allowed to perform the genetic alterations needed for the prisoners. Besides, they held all the patents for the chemical processes. They held all the patents, and Doddson's legislation assured them there would be no competition in this area. A simple boardroom suggestion by a 'woke' board member, to the effect of, "wouldn't it be nice if we were all the same skin color; there would be no more discrimination." Another board member had a more sinister idea and would have a talk with the senior scientist down in the lab. Thus began a very successful experiment that would blend well with current legislation in Washington. Doddson would create a monopoly for Genetic Tech, and it would stay that way through an act of Congress, just another quid-pro-quo that would enhance Doddson's coffers.

It was easy to see in light of the ever-burgeoning federal deficit. Over two hundred million for the Justice Department back in 09 had now ballooned to two hundred billion dollars in only ten years. The public would fully accept the change in the judicial system and the Penal Code. For years, the public had been outraged about the extremely liberal treatment the prisoners received: exercise rooms, flat-screen TVs, and even some private accommodations. And ever-increasing liberalism in the form of reduced bail for wanton crimes. Criminals were back on the street before the police even finished their paperwork.

When healthcare was nationalized, it was the most expensive peacetime legislation ever presented in America. It was also the worst medical service ever delivered to the public. However, for those with no medical coverage, it was certainly better than nothing, but barely. The number of people out of work added to those working but without coverage added again to those working but paying higher and higher premiums equaled a considerable majority. At this time, any legislation labeled a saving that was to be used to bolster both the medical benefits and Social Security would sail through Congress without a hitch.

Doddson's prison system overhaul plan saved billions of dollars and aided the enhancement and extension of the life of Social Security.

Chapter 4

"This is a really great Party, Donald!"

"Thanks, Henry. I'm glad you could make it." Senator Doddson said, trying to remember how much Henry Manchin and his corporation, Bloodwood Security, had contributed to his campaign.

Chris, the senator's aide, saw the senator wrinkle his brow and knew what he was thinking.

"250K," Chris whispered into Doddson's ear as he nonchalantly passed by the senator. Doddson was stunned for a minute, thinking the boy must be a mind reader.

Now, with that knowledge, Doddson knew he could pump Henry Stanforth for more of a contribution, and they began conversing. Doddson for more money, but Henry wanted the senator's ear for a proposal he and his executive team had cooked up.

For years the public had wanted more stringent persecution of lawbreakers and less public funds to incarcerate those criminals. Some people on the executive board of Bloodwood had developed a plan to do just that. They had also been advised of a new chemical process at Genetic Tech Corporation that was remarkable but useless for all intents and purposes until it was combined with the ultimate incarceration plan.

Before the night was over, Henry would donate an additional 10 million dollars, and Doddson assured him that his plan would come to fruition very quickly, and they would both reap great rewards from the deal.

The following day Henry was at the office early. He went to the lab to check on Floyd. The now completely blue chemist had been given regular living quarters and a new laboratory at the Bloodwood Headquarters. This made things easier for Floyd under his unique physical condition. It also kept the prying eyes of the public at bay.

After having talked to Doddson, it became apparent, at least in Henry's mind, that Floyd could never be allowed in public or anywhere for that matter. This problem would have to be dealt with very soon. The company had special employees to tend to this business.

Chapter 5

After a short and speedy trial, one in which the prosecutor laid out a weak case at best, but the defense attorney offered little or no rebuttal, and a jury rendered a beleaguered but quick opinion, the convict was sent for his painless genetic augmentation. The procedure took only ten minutes, but the results became very apparent in about four hours. Four hours and ten minutes later, Peter Rogan was escorted to an unmarked police van and driven to the edge of the woods of the National Forest. There, next to a tall willow, he was unchained and stood next to the van. Finally, the sentencing administrator spoke the last words of the court.

"Peter Rogan, you are hereby released to Nature. You have no rights. For your crimes, you have been expelled from our society. The constitution no longer protects you. Do you understand the sentence as I have stated it?" The administrator waited for Peter's reply.

"I'm not entirely clear as to what's happening. Are you telling me I'm free to go? Right?" Peter said.

"In a way, yes, you *are* free to go. But you are not free to engage in society nor leave the boundaries of this forest. You are not now, nor ever will be again, protected by the laws of this country", the administrator answered.

"It's still unclear," Peter said, trying to stall his inevitable release.

Regardless of the circumstances that he knew were coming, he felt at least a little protected by the two guards.

"Let me put it another way, as of this second, these men or I may beat you to within an inch of your life or even outright kill you without any legal consequence. Therefore, I suggest you take your leave into these woods immediately," the administrator explained in no uncertain terms.

Peter looked at his own hands. They were dark blue, where normally they were white and pale, and the reality of the trial and subsequent sentencing gripped him for the first time. He looked at the guards, saw their balled-up fists, and the malignant smile on their faces, and decided not to tempt fate any further. He turned and began running into the woods.

He stopped to catch his breath a quarter mile into the densely wooded forest. He rolled up the sleeve of his prison jumpsuit and saw the dark blue skin running up his arm. He pulled the front of his jumpsuit open to see his chest, waist, and genitals; they were all the same dark blue. A light spring rain started falling, and he tucked himself under a nearby maple tree. The reality of the situation was now setting into his brain. He was on his own, with no food, no money, no shelter, just the clothes on his back and the shoes on his feet. This is inhumane, he thought. But who could he complain to? Nobody! He remembered when the law had changed. The federal debt had been carried on the backs of the population so long that the electorate had revolted. The first change to save money and relieve debt came with the systematic dismantling of the prison system. He had thought at the time it certainly wouldn't affect him. And, like many others, didn't think about the consequences that might follow. He was a decent, hard-working citizen, paid most of his taxes like everyone else, and a little drug deal shouldn't carry a significant penalty. So why should he worry about this? Instead, the pain of his misguided indifference and lack of knowledge of the changes taking place was now welling up inside him, and he passed out under the tree.

The sun had been set for some time when Peter first woke up. It was chilly, and he pulled the small collar of his jumpsuit up around his neck as he sat up, leaning against the tree trunk. This is all he has, this jumpsuit and his shoes, nothing more. So, I'm going to die, and for what, selling a little dope, well, not really selling it but just not paying taxes on it, Yeah, that amounted to a lot of taxes, but Christ, I didn't think it was that big of a deal. It wasn't like those guys back in 09 or 10 that cheated all those people out of all their money, their life savings in some cases, with Ponzi schemes.

There was nothing more he could do. He listened to the sounds of the forest. A twig breaking here leaves rustling there. His heart was pounding. There was no moon, and the sky was cloudy, which made the forest so dark he couldn't see his hand in front of him.

Chapter 6

Doddson was gratified that ten more years had gone by without a hitch, no longer worrying about term limits. The prison reform and penal code changes had gone smoothly and been sucked up by the public and greatly appeased their mob bloodlust. The same scam had been pulled on the public a decade ago; Taxpayer money saved banks while the banking executives got bonuses. A great tactic, he thought, diverts attention and allows Congress to get away with just about anything. He had, in fact, made himself the hero he wanted to be.

The public majority allowed Habeas Corpus to be suspended ten years ago. With taxes at eighty percent, repealing cruel and unusual punishment was easy. The American public knew less and less about government history as each year passed. Their neighbors put down what few dissenters came along, and local officials were readily inclined to make the problem maker's addresses known unless they promised to shut their mouths. Ridicule by social media sites was a great form of fake information and denial. These social sites were heavily infiltrated and influenced by government bodies.

Getting the proper amount of backing for any bill was a little tricky. A deal here, a deal there, and some reciprocity being the sharpest knife causing the deepest cut. Amendments to the bill were not a problem. It's done all the time. You just had to know the most opportunistic time for the submission. Doddson knew the timing better than anyone on the hill.

Chapter 7

Peter Rogan woke with the sun in his eyes. He was sore, hungry, thirsty, and cold. He got up slowly, his body aching from sleeping against the tree all night. When he ran into the woods, he remembered the sun was at his back. Now he would walk toward the sun, never to return to the place of his release into the wild.

Peter had walked for miles. He had no idea where he was and may have been walking in circles. Suddenly, he heard shouting up ahead. His first reaction was to crouch down. But instead, he moved toward the noise, throwing caution to the wind and allowing nervous curiosity to direct his actions. Then, ducking down behind some thick bushes and crawling to a better vantage point, he could see another man, wearing jeans and a white t-shirt and appeared to have dark blue skin, like himself. The man was being surrounded by five young white men, all carrying dark-stained baseball bats. Peter remained perfectly still, horrified; he watched as the man turned in circles, desperately trying to confront his assailants. Then, with his back toward one of them, a bat came down on the convict's head. The man fell to the ground, arms crossed over his head, screaming in pain.

Other bats came from all directions; the man's screams turned to grunts and moans as he lay on the road. Broken bones started to protrude through his skin, and then his head broke open. Like a cracked egg, his brain matter spilled out onto the highway. The man's flinching had stopped now. The bats stopped as well. No fun in hitting a dead guy.

A helicopter whose engine could barely be heard had pulled up and hovered overhead as the beating ended. The five young men looked up but were without fear or apprehension. Having finished their perverted entertainment, they strolled away from the corpse, laughing and wiping blood from their hands and faces. The helicopter stayed a few more minutes, peeled off, and left the area. They radioed a report of another execution to the main office. The only cost to the system would be the cleanup crew that was sent to the location.

Still frozen with fear, Peter remained motionless. It wasn't, but a few minutes later, a green pickup pulled up, and two men jumped out. They were dressed in dark green uniforms. In large letters, the side of the truck read US Forest Sanitation. They walked up to the body; one of the men knelt down and was going to feel for a pulse and realized the futility of it. The two of them then hefted up the body by the arms and legs and swung it into the truck's bed like a sack of potatoes.

They got out some brooms and a can of liquid. Together they poured the fluid on the road and began using the brooms to clean the bloody area. More solution to rinse, then one of them said, "Clean enough, a good rain will take care of the rest, let's go." Throwing the can and brooms in the bed of the truck, they got in and drove away.

Pete stood transfixed by the scene he had just witnessed. He trembled; he wept. Was this his fate, he thought?

"Hey dumbass, youse betta get away from da road." Pete turned around so fast his legs crossed, and he tripped over himself. Then, looking up, he saw another blue man, just like himself. However, this one was shorter and skinnier but dark blue, just the same.

Chapter 8

Approval points for Congressman Doddson were at their highest. As a result, he was approached by several colleagues and asked if he would consider throwing his hat in the ring for president.

"Well, I don't know. Maybe".

He tried his best to act coy about the invitation. Inside he was bursting. For years, he had thought about being the president, and subconsciously that's what drove him. He had often used the term, "If I were running this country, or If I were president," when starting a rant of one sort or another.

He had accumulated his wealth with insider trading, certainly not openly, but he knew what legislation would lead to which companies to be more lucrative. His assistant Chris would have the appropriate family member make the proper stock purchase. He had also married into a great deal of money, like many others in politics, and would do things to keep and increase the family's wealth. Wealthy families seemed to gravitate to the Washington circle. Money was power, and power was everything. He was sure his offshore accounts, growing since he made the prison deals, would stay well concealed. In addition, now he had more backing and the party war chests.

Chapter 9

The newly arrived convict looked down at the clumsy new inmate and said, "gets up stupid, let's go. Youse outfit is so clean I figer you're a newbie. Soes I'll give ya a break, come on wit me before da chopper comes back."

Peter, not knowing what else to do, got up and followed the man as he was told at least he had not been threatened buy this new figure in his life. They walked briskly for the better part of half an hour with the sun off to their right.

Stopping finally, the con turned to Peter and said, "Wees in a safe spot fer now. Da names Eddie, youses new right?"

"Yeah, I'm Peter, Peter Rogan; they put me out here yesterday."

"Last names has no meanin out here. Peter, ya say? I'll just calls ya Pete; any problems wit dat?"

"No, Pete's fine. How long have you been here? Who were those guys on the road? Who's in the helicopter? Where exactly are we?"

"Whoa..."! Eddie said putting up his hands.

"Hold on, dude. Let me startch ya out right." Eddie said, shaking his head.

"Here's da deal." He started. "I only been here a few monts, so ders plenty I don't know. But somebody laid it down fer me when I foist got here, so I'll lay it out fer youse."

"If ya group up wit more den tree, day start droppen tear gas on yur ass. Sometimes, day drops da gas just fur fun to watch youse run and choke." Eddie looked at Pete's expression and thought, what a dope.

"Are youse listenen ta me, Petey" Eddie injected. "I'm not goin over dis again. I'm serious" Eddie waited for a reply."

"Yes, yes, I'm listening, but it seems so unreal," Peter answered.

"Well, it's real alright. Da choppers gots infrared radar, so ya can't never hide. Well, anyway, ders only three rules: one, no more den tree in a group. Two, Stays away from da road. And numba tree. Die!"

Eddie elaborated that inside the road, you were probably safe being patrolled only by the guards and some punks, but at the road and beyond the law was 'that there was no law.' Those grounds were patrolled by and owned by anyone who had the balls and weapons and the nerve to use them, remembering that there would be no consequences to their actions as long as the victims were Blue.

"Thanks for the advice, Ed," Peter said apprehensively and continued. "But where is the guy who taught you."

"Well, he was my partner fer a while. But I gots him close enough to da road for da punks to take care of; we was sleepin ta geda which was natural an all ta keeps warm and all, but he wanted ta get a little too friendly. Understand?" Ed said, eyeing Peter to see if he got the real gist of the explanation.

"Remember ders only the tree rules no more no less. So that means I could kill you, and no one cares, just like the punks you saw. Cept they can go home at night." Eddie finished.

That left Pete in a total state of depression. Unfortunately, those three rules seemed to be all too true, and rule number three was becoming more welcome with each passing day.

Chapter 10

Doddson eased through the handshaking; he was an expert and throwing compliments at the right people came easy. Many of his peers were sucking up to him as well, and he was sucking up to others. His power was well known, and alliances were forthcoming. Chris, Doddson's aide, made sure the food and drinks were of the highest quality and steadily brought into the party. Chris had been Doddson's aide for ten years, ever since the prison deal. He knew more than the congressman gave him credit, and Chris always had his ears open and remembered everything anyone said.

Doddson, with a great smile and an equally great line of bullshit, managed to bring in several million in campaign contributions that night. A few more parties like this and I'll be ready for a nomination fight, he thought to himself.

Chapter 11

Eddie and Peter had walked a few more miles in silence. Peter didn't want to press Eddie too much but needed to get more of the picture.

"Ed, what about women? Are there any in the woods here?"

"I've seen some gals in here der ain't many. But most, what I hear, hook up pretty quick wit da biggest guy day can find. Maybees days feel safer. I's pretty sure der must be moah but maybe day puts em in a different place."

"What do you do to keep warm or stay dry,"

"Look here, Pete, I told you ders only tree rules. If you need to stays dry, find a good tick evergreen tree. It's early summer, near as I can tell. I almost froze to death when I got here, but that's what a partner is for, so long as he doesn't get too friendly. Understand, Petey boy."

Ed stared him in the eyes for extra emphasis.

"I got it, I got it, really!" Peter exclaimed.

Pretty satisfied at this point, Ed knew that Peter would not get too friendly and continued his sermon.

"So far as anyting else, ya know as much as me. So far, I know what kin be eaten and where ders some water. I had a fire once but rubbing sticks together will wear ya right out. This here walking cane I'm carryin is a bit sharp, and I managed to kill a few critters, but eat'n em raw takes a bit of doing."

Pete would have vomited about now, but his stomach was too empty.

"Maybe between the two of us, we can get a campfire going," Pete said.

"Is there any water around here, Eddie?" Pete asked.

"Sure, Petey, I was on my way dare whens I founds you. Follow me!"

Another hundred yards and they came across a small creek. The first thing Ed did was look carefully around to make sure no one else was in the area. He didn't like taking his eyes off his surrounding but had to to get water. Next, he lay down by the stream and splashed water on his face. Then dipped his head into the water and gulped hardily.

Pete watched Ed and then looked at the water. It looked clean enough, but the algae swayed in the current, and he saw a small creature scuttle away as Ed splashed more water on his face and head.

Pete bent down close to the water and scooped a little into his mouth. There was undoubtedly no chlorine taste, making it seem fresh somehow. Nevertheless, he got down like Ed did and drank readily.

Ed stopped him and said, "dats enough fer now. It'll take some time fer yur body to gets use ta what's floating around in dare." Pete looked up at Ed and shook his head in agreement.

Later Pete ran into yet another inmate, a tall, large built man. Thinking he would be as cordial as Eddie, he stopped to say hi and maybe gain a little more insight into his situation. Much to his regret, the conversation was short and painful. The new inmate was larger than Pete and quickly grabbed him by the neck with one hand while plummeting him in the face with the other hand. Pete was stunned and tried desperately to avoid the flying fist while kicking at the other man.

Fortunately, Eddie came from behind a large tree and, with his cane in hand, drove the pointed end deep into the back of the neck of Pete's assailant. The man became stiff, released Pete from his grip, and then fell limp to the ground. Pete, now on the ground holding his neck and gasping for breath, recovered enough to ask Eddie what he had done to evoke the stranger's wrath.

Eddie looked at Pete with pity. "I guess in youse case, we has ta make a fort rule. You know, like da numba forwah." Eddie said holding up four fingers. "Always be aware of your surroundings and expect the woist from strangers."

Pete, still rubbing his neck, shook his head in affirmation of the newly created rule.

"But what did he want from me,"

"It's hard ta say, Petey, maybe your shoes, maybe there's something in youse pockets like food, maybe he just wants to have his way with you, if ya knows what I mean,"

"But I have nothing, nothing at all, well maybe the shoes, but I don't think they would fit him."

"Ferget about it, maybe he just wanted to kill you, or maybe he just wanted you ta kill him, in witch case he gots his wish, and now his pain is over."

"Let's get a move on in case he has any friends around. Check his pockets and take his shoes and jumpsuit; they may be good trading and you might want to double up your clothes if gets colder."

"But Eddie, we can't just leave his body here."

"Really, gives me a reason why we can't?"

Pete thought for a minute and then took the shoes and jumpsuit. He rolled the clothes and used the shoelaces to tie it all together. He could use the roll as a pillow until he needed it for warmth.

"Ok, Eddie, lead the way."

As they left this area heading for a more desolate part of the forest, Pete looked around, far away he could see more orange jumpsuits, mostly in pairs. He wasn't sure if he just didn't notice the others before or if Eddie had led them into a more populated area. The National Forest was big but the amount of prisoners being sent here must be putting a strain on the land use.

Pete asked Eddie why he was seeing more inmates now than before.

"Well, Pete I'm not entirely sure but I tink we're closer to a large lake then we were before. It's late summer and the water gives a little relief from da heat, and you can wash up, and most of all we's a lot farder from da road and darefor from da punks dat patrol it. Dares also da food drop."

"Wait, what? A food drop what's that?"

"Pete day can't just sends us out here wit out no food. Dares soyten areas weres day drops food. Da choppers drop it and it splatters everywheres. Day're small blocks of protein I tink. Like s an over sized candy bar."

"Well lets get some, where do we go?"

"We goes nowhere we waits and if we sees a drop and it's close enough we run, grab some bars and keep runnin. Udders are watchen too, it's foist come foist served but dat don't mean it cant be taken away from ya an dat leaves ya wit the mice and moles."

Chapter 12

Doddson did well in the debates, reminding everyone how much money his legislation had saved with the prison bill. He was a brilliant speaker and knew what the people wanted to hear. He debated in school, winning almost every contest he entered. This was no different from all the campaigning he had done to get where he was today.

Donald Doddson was on the way to becoming his party's candidate for President of the United States. The opposing parties had only a sorrowful list of opponents with little to offer. The primaries within his own party came and went, and Doddson was victorious, although his opponents were really there in name only. They realized all too soon how popular he was and how far ahead he was in any pole.

The other parties had their final choices on stage and the Doddson charisma, within minutes, made them all look like fools. These debates would go on for months, and he felt he would have no problem shining like the star he thought he was. A few of the candidates dropped out shortly after the first debate, many of the others fell like leaves on a autumn tree.

Chapter 13

Peter and Eddie traveled the woods for the better part of the summer. Pete had found some sharp stones and a hardy branch; he managed to hone a nice spear that seconded as a walking cane. Peter learned what was edible and what was not and had, on occasion, speared a few rodents and an occasional fish. However, Peter's physical condition wouldn't tolerate most of it. He continued to lose weight and vomiting, and dysentery were taking their toll.

"Eddie, I can't deal with this much longer."

"Pete, I told ja what da laws are, and if you keeps dis up, you're look'n at law number tree."

"No, I can't believe this is what it's all about."

"Well, it is Petey. Maybe youse got some udder idea?"

"Yes, we need to get to a town to get some food, some real food." Peter whimpered.

"Der ain't no way, ders too many obstacles, da choppers, da punks, and who knows what else." Eddie hollered.

"I gotta try, Eddie, I gotta try!"

Eddie thought Peter was a pretty good guy. They had become friends over the past few months, and now Eddie felt sorry for Peter. He saw him losing weight and realized he wouldn't make it through the winter. He wondered if even he would make it in the next winter season.

"Eddie, I've been watching the helicopters and counting the minutes between sightings. Counting the seconds in my head. They come from different directions, but there is a common recurring time gap." Peter explained and went on. "Ed, how close can we get to the road without being gassed?"

"I don't know, Petey, maybe 200 yards on a good day."

In desperation, Pete laid out his plan to Eddie. They would, of course, wait until dark. The choppers flew in 18-minute intervals, but in the evening, the interval was 22 minutes; maybe a shift change or a refueling occurred. It didn't matter, that was the longest period between copters, and it happened every night at the same time.

They would wait two hundred yards from the road. Then, when the copter left the area, they would sprint the distance to the road, cross, and then keep going another three hundred yards. 1800 feet seemed like a long way. Neither man was in the greatest shape, but both were highly motivated.

Night fell; Pete and Eddie sat two hundred yards off the road, away from the copter radar, and waited. Then, as the nine o'clock chopper left, the two men ran the two hundred yards to the road looked around for any punks and seeing none kept going. After another two hundred yards, they saw a winding road and, panting heavily, decided to rest after they crossed it. Eddie led the way; being smaller and wiry and in slightly better shape, he was thirty yards ahead of Pete when he started to cross the road and was hit by a small, fast-moving red convertible. Pete saw Eddie's body fly off the car's windshield and heard the screeching tires as the car came to a halt. Eddie could hear a

woman screaming in panic. He laid low under some bushes to
see what would happen next.

Chapter 14

Doddson's campaign went to every major city. In each city, he made a showing, gathering large crowds and deafening cheers. The major news companies began their deep vetting, trying desperately to find dirt and try as they may, being unsuccessful. Doddson had gone to great lengths to ensure he remained squeaky clean over the years. Only he and his aide were aware of where the skeletons were buried. Doddson assumed they were buried deep enough and that Chris, being well compensated, much more than any regular aide, would keep the skeletons buried deep.

Chris, his aide for many years, saw the time coming to parley his knowledge, compensation or no his stepbrother had gotten into trouble, and now there was no place to turn. He felt guilty that the things he had done had brought about changes in the penal code which led to the prosecution of a member of his family.

Chris and Peter played together as children and were as close to each other as brothers ever could be. Unfortunately, they hadn't been in touch with each other except for holiday family gatherings for several years.

Chris remembered Peter as a risk taker, and normally anything that Peter might have been guilty of would be considered a misdemeanor. However, the new legislation has moved many misdemeanors up to felonies and his stepbrother was a victim of those new changes. Chris knew the worst was coming and he knew how to change the outcome.

Chapter 15

Chris sat in front of the governmental investigator. His eyes darted around the sterile room; a frosted window let in minimal light. The frost on the window seemed equivalent to the investigator's tone and demeanor.

"Tell me what you know," the investigator started.

"I know Doddson's accounts and their locations and their amounts."

"That's not news; we know about his accounts too."

"No, I don't think you know about *all* of his accounts or of *how* he filled them." Chris came sternly back.

The investigator's eyebrows lifted quizzically, and his frosty tone became more serious.

"You know you're talking about a presidential candidate," said the investigator.

"Yes, I know who he is and what he is, and I have a deal I want to make," Chris retorted.

"We usually don't make deals, but what's your pitch," the investigator continued.

Chris looked him in the eye. "My stepbrother was convicted of tax evasion and drug charges."

"Those are pretty serious offenses, now a day. So, what's your deal?"

"He was sentenced to genetic altering and released to the National Forest; I need to get him out of there," Chris complained.

The investigator looked down and shook his head.

"I'll see what I can do, but it depends on your information," the investigator said with a straight face, knowing he was about to lie to the young congressional assistant.

The investigator realized what Chris was asking was impossible. Genetic changes were irreversible, as was the sentence itself. So, he would have to lie to Chris to squeeze any information out of him.

As he knew it, Chris relayed the entire story: all the accounts, money, contracts, kickbacks, and payoffs. It was extensive and extremely well hidden. Chris had been at the top of the congressman's loyal associates, having worked for him for more than ten years. However, to have a member of his family sentenced in Federal Court under this new penal system was more than he could take. He knew this was indeed a death sentence.

The investigator smiled and thanked Chris for his cooperation. He told him to go on with his everyday routine. He told him he would be in touch and soon. The smile continued on his face after Chris had left. He had never liked Doddson. This was a final assurance that he would never become president. He also knew that Chris, whether he knew it or not, had destroyed his career, and worse, he would never see his stepbrother again.

Chapter 16

Pete watched as the couple in the small sports car argued. He saw them on the phone. He thought for a moment about stealing the car but didn't want to give away his escape. It didn't take but a few moments before the police showed up, and Pete hunkered down into the bushes even further. He had heard the chopper returning and hoped he was far enough from the perimeter to stay hidden. So far, he was lucky. Eddie, however, was not as fortunate.

Pete could hear the police in the bushes on the other side of the road shout, "Over here, it's a body... and it's dead".

Pete bowed his head in respect for Eddie. Now Pete was alone in uncharted territory, and most of his poorly thought-out plan had turned to shit. It was an hour or two before the tow truck arrived, and Pete slept fitfully under the bushes. The tow truck made enough noise to wake him, and he watched as the car was towed away. The owners, still arguing, were in the cab of the truck.

Pete decided that the terrain was the same as the prison forest, and as long as he stayed away from the roads, he might be safe. When morning came, he got up and started to explore. He hoped he could find an unoccupied house where he could get some food and clothing.

Chapter 17

Doddson arrived early to his office, which was expected; what was not normal was the number of people standing in front of his office. A man dressed in a black suit holding a badge introduced himself as agent Stanley Mezelko of the FBI. As the officer began speaking, cameras clicked, and microphones on the ends of outstretched arms appeared everywhere pointing at Doddson's face.

"Congressman Doddson, you are under arrest for bribery, tax evasion, and Use of official position or office for personal gain. Offering, soliciting or accepting things of value from a lobbyist, subordinate of a lobbyist, or principal. Use or disclosure of confidential information gained in the course or by reason of their position for personal financial gain. Voting in matters with a financial interest. You have the right to remain silent; you have the right to an attorney...."

Doddson heard the words from the FBI agent and saw the smile on his aide's face across the room. The words spoken to him became garbled. In earlier times, this would have been a 2 to 20-year sentence with a stiff fine, but now, as so many others had learned, lesser sentences turn into class one felonies which meant the Forest, which was in itself a death sentence.

Doddson stood while his hands were cuffed. Still staring at Chris and wondering why he had not cultivated a deeper relationship with his aide. Perhaps he should have cut Chris in for a percentage. Although, as Doddson was led out of his office, he was still trying to figure out how he could have avoided this, regret maybe, but remorse was not on his mind.

Chris thought only of his stepbrother, who would soon be back home.

Chapter 18

Pete Rogen was moving slowly in the new environment. It was generally the same landscape, yet new as far as he was concerned. Eddie's walking cane was lost during the accident, so no mice or mole would be skewered today. Pete was starving and thirsty.

Over the next rise, Pete saw a small house and approached slowly. He saw no lights inside and no vehicles outside. He went around to the back, looking in the windows as he passed them. The back door was locked; he waited, listening for any movement inside. With no noise forthcoming, he broke the window, reached inside, and turned the locking pin. The door opened quietly.

The inside of the house was warm, and Pete felt good, almost normal. He entered the kitchen and went straight for the fridge. It was well stocked, with meat, vegetables, and plenty of leftovers, cold but all cooked. He gorged himself. He realized he didn't check the remainder of the house and walked softly through the remaining rooms while eating a chicken leg. Nobody was here.

After eating, he returned to the bedroom and found clothes that, to his surprise, fit well. He found an excellent cold-weather coat hanging in the back of the closet; it, too, fit well. Next, he used the bathroom and washed up. Scrubbing as hard as he could, but the blue, as you can imagine, would not wash out. Nevertheless, he had not felt this good or clean since he was dropped off in the Forest many months ago.

He found a backpack and filled it with food and bottled water. Looking out in the yard, he saw no one around. He took the queue to leave. He followed the driveway a half mile down to the road it intersected. Pete backed up about fifty yards and started walking parallel to the road in a direction he felt would take him away from the prison forest.

Chapter 19

Doddson's three-day trial went smoothly for the prosecutor. The evidence was overwhelming as well as irrefutable. In another time the trial would have dragged on for months, but under the new laws speedy trials were required. On the fourth day, the jury returned a verdict in less than fifteen minutes. Sentencing would take place early the following week.

Doddson had been allowed to wear a suit and tie for the trial. The defense thought it might positively influence the jury, he did look remarkable, and the suit was from his own collection, all handmade and tailored to perfection. It didn't help. The jury members easily recognized that this type of wealth accumulation on a congressional salary could only have come from all the things the prosecutor had said he had done.

His looks did not help him.

Doddson was sitting in a holding cell waiting to be transferred from the court back to his federal cell to await sentencing. Looking around, he realized no one was on observation duty; this was highly unusual, and someone had made a grievous error of not taking his tie away from him. Doddson climbed up and stood on the thin headboard of the bunk. He secured one end of his tie to the ceiling fan and the other end around his neck. He thought to himself how great life had been and how fast things could turn to shit. At any rate, he resolved he would not be subject to his own prison scheme. He calmly stepped off the bed to meet his maker.

When Donald L Doddson awoke, he found himself in a hospital bed. His head ached, and he could feel the bandages around his head. He was informed that due to his weight, the ceiling fan had come apart from the ceiling and landed squarely on his skull, knocking him unconscious and in a coma for a week. He was also informed that his sentence had been given and he had already been altered; he would be taken to the Forest within a few hours.

Doddson sat up and looked at his hands and arms. Pulling the sheets back and lifting his hospital gown, he saw that he was, in fact, all blue, head to toe.

They would come for him soon and take him away. He could not let this happen. Being in a coma, no one had thought to secure him to the bed. Only feet away was the window, and Donald ran toward it and crashed through the glass. He fell four feet ten inches to the ground. Amazingly he received only a few cuts and scratches. Several men helped him get up, but instead of returning him to the hospital bed, they helped him into the waiting prison van. He was screaming as the van pulled away.

Chapter 20

For Pete to think that no one in the prison system knew he was missing was a little naïve. This wasn't the first time someone tried to escape, and by this time in history, the blue skin of a convict was all too easy to recognize. Pete had put a hat on and covered his face with a scarf and dark glasses he had found at the house. He also found some gloves. With this disguise, he thought he was safe.

The house owner returned from work that evening and found the broken window of the back door. He backed away from the house while calling the police.

Pete, now miles away, stopped his arduous trek to appease his growing hunger. Crouched down by a large tree, he ate. He stared at his hands, his blue hands. He stared at them for a long time. Pete then realized that no matter what he did, he could never change the color of his skin. The plan was foolproof. No matter where he went, he could never rejoin society; he could never live a normal life. In the distance, he could hear dogs barking and baying as if they had just picked up a scent. He remembered he had left his prison jumpsuit in the house. Pete got up and started to run.

He ran through the woods for a mile or more. Now out of breath, Pete came to the edge of a cliff. He thought it must be several hundred feet or more to the bottom. He could also hear the dogs getting closer. There's nowhere to run and nowhere to hide. When they find him, and they will, they could return him to the edge of the Forest like the first day he arrived, or they could just beat him to death right here and now, and no one would care. No disguise would prevent him from being found.

Pete stared down over the cliff's edge and then at his blue hands and arms. He remembered rule number three. "I'm not going back." He said out loud as he leaned over the edge farther than his balance could recover. As he fell, the satisfaction of freedom overtook his fear. He closed his eyes tightly, he thought about his family and friends and about his stepbrother, he hoped Chris would understand the fate Peter had chosen. The end came a few seconds later. This was, in fact, a scenario that the government plan had predicted. Nature and suicide would keep the inmate population in check and not add to the expense of the prison system.

Chapter 21

The prison system works well; old prisons have been sold and turned into factories, offices, or just razed for subdivisions or shopping malls.

The nation was ecstatic about the change, and crime rates have dropped dramatically, especially gang crimes. Liberal prosecutors had long ago been unseated, and most had been subject to the current laws. Petty theft and dereliction of duty was added to the penal code as a felony, and all felons went to the forest. As soon as the rumors about what happens in the forest got around, attitudes changed. No bail, but a speedy trial and then the cane or, if your nightmare comes true, the forest, nothing in between.

If you're bad, you get spanked with a cane.

If you're really bad, and the "really" part is constantly being redefined, that's another story. The forest perimeter has been expanded to accommodate more inmates due to penal code changes. The forest takes lives, sure, but it's cheap to run. The electorate loves it. The only early release program is an obituary; if they even find your body. Once the skin is turned, there is no reprieve. There is no retrial; there is no "I'm sorry we made a mistake." Nobody is black, and nobody is white. They're all just Blue.

Lofty prisons big and tall,
Lofty Prisons short and small.
No money for prisons,
that's the rub; the hue stays on,
even when you scrub.
Gone are now the prison walls,
gone also are the rooms and halls.
Just a tree or shrub survives,
you work like hell to stay alive.

The crime you do may be just slight,
And if it is, the cane will bite.
But if it's more that crime you do,
Beware your fate; they'll turn you Blue.

Reference United States Penal Code, July 2050

Don't miss out!

Visit the website below and you can sign up to receive emails whenever J.J. Smiley publishes a new book. There's no charge and no obligation.

https://books2read.com/r/B-A-NBSE-CIWDC

BOOKS 2 READ

Connecting independent readers to independent writers.

Also by J.J. Smiley

All That Remains
Coven; Short Stories of Sci-fi and Fantasy
The Tree
Girls
Blue Man
Run!

About the Author

Disappointed with titles that I read or watched in the theatre, it was time to write my own adventures. Just writing for personal pleasure at first and then publishing, has now become a joyful pastime.

My wife who is always watching my back convinced me to go to press.